Mayfield Crossing

VAUNDA MICHEAUX NELSON grew up in a small town in Pennsylvania, the youngest of five children. She is the author of *Always Gramma*, a picture book. *Mayfield Crossing* is her first novel. She currently lives in Albuquerque, New Mexico, with her husband Drew, who is also a writer.

Mayfield Crossing

VAUNDA MICHEAUX NELSON

AN AVON  CAMELOT BOOK

AVON BOOKS
A division of
The Hearst Corporation
1350 Avenue of the Americas
New York, New York 10019

Copyright © 1993 by Vaunda Micheaux Nelson
Published by arrangement with G.P. Putnam's Sons
Library of Congress Catalog Card Number: 92-10564
ISBN: 0-380-72179-1
RL: 4.8

First Avon Camelot Printing: January 1994

CAMELOT TRADEMARK REG. U.S. PAT. OFF. AND IN OTHER COUNTRIES, MARCA REGISTRADA,
HECHO EN U.S.A.

Printed in the U.S.A.

OPM 10 9 8 7

*For Olive Batch Micheaux
and Norris Edward Micheaux, Jr.,
my mother and father*

Mayfield Crossing

Prologue

Papa once said being different is both a blessing and a curse. He said people who are different give ordinary people something to talk about so they don't get bored with having to live with themselves all the time. I laughed at that, and so did Billie and Mama. Then he said that people who are different make things happen; they change things.

"What if people like things the way they are?" I asked.

Papa's forehead wrinkled as he lowered his eyebrows and said, "That's when the blessing becomes a curse."

He didn't say more about it, and I never asked him to explain. But since then, I've been finding out for myself— the bad and the good.

I suppose it really started a long time ago, with Harry. But I didn't begin to understand until last September. The day Dillon's father brought home their brand-new 1960 Studebaker. The day we played our last ball game together before things changed.

❧ *Chapter One*

It was hot and dusty, and the woods that surrounded the Crossing were still mostly green, but some of the trees were touched with red or orange or yellow. I hadn't seen much beyond those woods and the town of Mayfield Crossing, none of us had.

Tomorrow we will, I thought, catching a perfect pitch.

"Strike two," I said, keeping the cool in my voice but feeling like jumping clean to the sky, both for the strike and for tomorrow.

Billie didn't even crack a smile. He knew the game wasn't over. He was concentrating on his next pitch.

My brother had some arm. He could throw a ball so hard it stung your hand right through the mitt. We needed a pitch like that now. The score was tied at six, they had runners on second and third, there were two outs, and Luke Cleary was up.

I slid my catcher's mask away from my face.

"Keep it on, Meg," Billie called in his protective way.

"Can't see," I yelled back, but flipped it down just the same.

"You're doin' fine," Luke said, taking a practice swing, his red hair reflecting the sunlight. "That was a good call. I shoulda swung."

That meant something, coming from Luke. He was eleven, two years older, and treating me like an equal. Luke was good. Real good. Most times, if he was on your team, you could plan on winning.

But we were lucky today. We had Fitch Sherman on our side. He was the king of double plays and loved playing shortstop, but, as usual, we only had four players on each team, so today he was covering between first and second base. His twin brother Owen was covering second and third. From where I was, it was like seeing double.

Owen was the fastest talker this side of the tracks, but he couldn't play baseball worth spit. Trouble was, Owen stuck to his brother like glue. It was common knowledge in Mayfield Crossing that if you planned anything with Fitch, you got the whole package. But Owen was all right. I'd eat a plateful of liver if I ever heard he told a lie.

"Take your time, Turner. Take your time," Owen called to Billie.

Dillon Wood was standing on the tree stump we used as second base, looking the other way, probably birdwatching. He was the best on foot in the Crossing, famous for stretching a double or even a triple out of a hit that'd only put most on first base. But it was Alice Cleary I was worried about.

She had her foot right on the edge of our third-base rock, ready to charge the instant Luke connected or I dropped a ball. Alice could steal a base fast as a jack rabbit, and she was known for blinding the catcher with dust on a slide. It hadn't rained in weeks, so already the dust was heavy, showing like powder on my brown arms. I tugged one of my pigtails, then threw it behind my shoulder. I knew I could catch, but I wasn't good under pressure.

"Come on, Lukey," Mo Cleary said from behind me. She was up next and standing on a log near home plate. Right then, I wished it was her on third base instead of Alice. Mo never stole a base in her life. Didn't think it was fair.

If Luke struck out, it would be the bottom of the ninth and our chance to break the tie and win the game. With school starting tomorrow, it would be the last game of the summer, so everybody wanted to win bad. A cloudburst with lightning and thunder couldn't have ended the game.

Luke held the bat like he planned to send the ball to Jupiter. But just as Billie threw his emergency pitch, a

5

slow curve ball we called the "Untouchable Turner," Dillon shouted, "Here comes Old Hairy!"

"Shoot," Billie said.

Luke dropped the bat and ran toward left field.

By the time I knew what had happened, the ball was safe in my glove and everybody was running. Running away from the dusty Mayfield School ball field, away from the game of the year, maybe the best short-handed game of our entire lives. But nobody cared who won anymore.

"Come on, Meg!" Billie yelled.

I picked up the bat and raced over third base after them. We all hid behind some bushes and, catching my breath, I watched Old Hairy come out of the woods behind first base and stroll onto the field.

Old Hairy wasn't really that old, but he was strange. He wore faded overalls and a plaid flannel shirt even though it was hot as blazes. And he had so many whiskers, he looked like a werewolf. Mama said he was "an original." But to Mayfield kids, he was a terror.

Old Hairy skipped up to home plate with a quick, light step, kind of like he was doing a soft-shoe dance. He moved his arms like he was swinging a bat, then started running around the bases.

"Man, he's crazy," Owen said.

"Yeah," Billie said, wiping sweat from his forehead

with his shirttail and keeping his eyes on Hairy, "but at least Old Hairy won't be crashing our games at the new school. He won't be able to find us."

I glanced across the field at the Mayfield schoolhouse. It was a sorry sight with the windows all boarded up. Tomorrow we were going to Parkview Elementary, a bigger school with kids from other neighborhoods. It had been nice, being in a small school, knowing everybody. But we'd heard that Parkview had a huge ball field with thick grass, and we were itching to try it out. And there would be lots more kids, so we'd be sure to have enough players to cover the field. Besides, at Mayfield Old Hairy was always coming around and breaking things up. We'd be safe from him at Parkview.

A loud whistle pierced the air. It was Mrs. Sherman calling for the twins.

"I'm not leavin' these bushes," Owen said. "Not 'til Old Hairy's outta here."

Mama'd be calling us in soon, too, and she'd be sore if we were late for supper because of Hairy.

She was funny about Old Hairy. She got mad at us for running away from him. I wondered if she'd think differently if she knew what we knew about Hairy—and about his hatchet.

We all stood closer together. I tugged my pigtail and hoped those years of Sunday School would pay off, but my mind was blank. I couldn't seem to remember even one of the hundreds of prayers I'd learned. I whispered "Amen" anyway, just in case *wanting* to say a prayer was as good as doing it and the Lord would come through after all.

As Hairy rounded third base and came past our hiding place, everybody ducked back behind the bushes. But I wasn't quick enough. Old Hairy looked dead at me and held his hand up. Mama would have wanted me to wave back, but I couldn't.

Luke pulled me down out of sight, then we all peeked out again, just as Hairy was running across home plate.

"Jeepers, I didn't know he could move like *that*," Luke whispered.

"He's pretty fast all right," I said, wondering if I could outrun him if I had to.

❧ *Chapter Two*

"We should've won by default," Alice insisted, standing on our back porch after supper, one hand on her hip. She combed the fingers of her other hand through her tangled red hair and said, "Our team was still willing to play." Alice was a serious player. She got real mad when things didn't go her way. But we understood. There are times when a person can't be held responsible.

"Come on, Alice," Mo said, her freckled hands folded on top of her head. "That wouldn't be right. Most of Billie's team had to leave. It could have been any of us called home."

"It was an even game," Billie said. He was sitting on the porch floor, his big, dark eyes—eyes like Papa's—focused on a rip in the knee of his overalls.

"Maybe," Alice went on. "But if it hadn't been for Old Hairy, we'd have whipped your tails."

"No way," Owen protested. "Billie was just about to strike out Luke the Duke."

Luke started to take his glasses off like he does when he's about to convince you of something.

But before he could, I cut in, "Nobody knows what would've happened."

"Right," Mo agreed. "Like Billie said, it was an even game."

Finally Alice plopped into a chair. "Okay. Okay. But we're gonna whip the tails off those Parkview kids when we play them."

Everybody laughed. Kids from the Crossing didn't fight much. Not for real. And when they did, the mad didn't stick.

"I wish he'd get here," Dillon said from the porch step. I don't think he'd heard a word about the game. He was waiting for his dad. The two of them were real close. He didn't have a mom. She died when he was five.

Today Mr. Wood was bringing home his first new car. It was a big deal for all of us. We were used to second-hand.

"Well, is it time yet?" Luke asked.

Dillon didn't answer. He strained his neck to see down the narrow blacktop road that crossed the railroad tracks. His yellow cowlick was standing up so straight it looked like it was straining to see, too. It would have been easier to watch from the front porch, but after Old Hairy showed up there one day last spring, we felt safer out back.

"Is it time yet?" Luke asked again.

"No," Dillon finally said. "Still, I wish he'd come."

We laughed. But I knew what he meant. Waiting is hard, whether it's for something bad like a report card, or something good like Christmas, or even something like going to Parkview School.

"I can't wait 'til tomorrow!" I blurted out. "Mama made me a new dress. It's blue plaid with a white collar."

"Grandma made dresses for Alice and me, too." Mo was excited. "The one I'm wearing tomorrow is green. Gram says I look good in green."

"I hate 'em," said Alice. "They're all frilly and starch-scratchy, like church clothes. How're we gonna play ball?"

"Billie's gonna wear a tie," I teased, nudging him with my elbow, hoping to get him riled.

"Am not." Billie flashed a look at me, then glanced around at everybody else. "Papa said other boys probably won't wear them and I might feel out of place. So Mama changed her mind."

"Our mom said there might be some people at Parkview who don't want us there, so there might be some trouble," Fitch said in a low voice. His eyes were serious. He and Owen had the same gray eyes and tight curls of black hair. But up close, it was easy to tell who was who.

"What kind of trouble?" I asked.

Fitch folded his arms in front of him. "I don't know, but Pop told us to mind our p's and q's, whatever that means."

"I guess we can do whatever we want to with the rest of the alphabet," Owen said, grinning.

That Owen. Fitch pretended to push him over the porch rail.

"I'm just glad we'll all be at the same school." Mo put her arm behind me on the porch swing.

When Mayfield School closed, some politicians divided the Crossing into north, south, east, and west sections and spread us around to different schools. Some kids were going to Liberty, Washington, or Riverside School. We were the east section and going to Parkview.

"What if they had drawn the dividing line right between our houses?" Mo said.

"I would have died!" I cried, hugging her closer.

Beep, beep!

"He's here!" Dillon said, so quiet I hardly heard. He practically flew off the steps, and we all charged after him.

Mr. Wood was waving out the car window as he pulled up in a shiny, willow-green station wagon. A 1960 Studebaker Lark. It was a clumsy-looking car with a sort of a fish-mouth grill. We had had wild dreams of a Lincoln

Continental with the "suicide" back doors that opened from the wrong end. But nobody was complaining about the Studebaker. It was the nicest car any of us had ever seen, except in pictures or from a distance.

"Oooooweee!" Dillon exclaimed, running around and around the car.

"I can see myself," Alice said, looking at her reflection in the chrome bumper.

"A star of a car," Owen sang.

"Can we have a ride?" Dillon asked, leaning in the window on the passenger side.

Mr. Wood smiled and said, "Sure, if it's all right with everyone's folks."

By now, our folks had heard the commotion and were gathering around the car.

"Nice," Papa said, nodding his head. "Nice."

Mama wiped her hands on her checked apron. Then she came over, reached in a window, and felt the soft green seats. "Mmmmm," she said, like she had tasted something real good.

"Can we? Can we go for a ride?" I begged, jumping up and down.

Billie looked up at Mama, his face asking the same thing.

She put her hand on top of my head to stop my jumping. "All right," she said, laughing, "but tomorrow is school, so when you get back, it's into the tub with both of you, then early to bed. Deal?"

"Deal!" Billie and I said together.

"But Meg first!" Billie added, running to get into the car. On a regular night, I might have argued, but tonight I was feeling so good I didn't care. Besides, I figured now I'd have something to bargain with on another night.

Everybody was allowed to go, but first, even though we'd already dusted each other off after the ball game, Mr. Wood made us do it again. Dust was flying everywhere, like when Mama beat rugs she'd hung over the clothesline.

Dillon sat up front with Alice. Fitch, Owen, and Billie got in the back seat. And Mo and I climbed into the wayback. As we pulled away, I heard Mrs. Cleary holler, "Can we have a turn tomorrow?"

"If the kids say it's okay," Mr. Wood called back, and we drove off down the road.

I'll remember that car ride until the day I die. The Crossing passed by the window—Mason's Drug Store, the Five and Ten, Keegan's Gas Station, the Dairy Queen. The radio blared "You Ain't Nothin' But a Hound Dog," with all of us singing like Elvis. And the smell . . . the smell was all newness.

❧ Chapter Three

It was me driving that car in my mind when Mama and Papa came to tuck us in.

Papa sat on Billie's bed and Mama sat on mine. "You two go right off to sleep now," Mama said, kissing both my cheeks. "No talking after lights out. You have a big day tomorrow."

Papa said something to Billie that I couldn't hear. Then he looked over and said, "Meg, remember you might not get to sit near Mo in your class tomorrow. If that happens, try to see it as a chance to get to know the other children, to make new friends."

"Yes, Papa."

Both he and Mama were quiet for a while. I could tell there was something else they wanted to say. I turned onto my side and pulled my knees up close to my chest.

"Mama," I said, breaking the silence. "Mrs. Sherman

told Fitch and Owen that some people at Parkview might not want us there. She said there could be trouble. Is that true?"

Mama looked over at Papa. "It's possible," she said. "Some people are uncomfortable with folks they don't know. Folks who may be a little different from them."

"You mean 'cause we're from Mayfield?"

"Partly, yes," Papa said, "but you may be the only Negro in your class. Billie, too."

So what? I wanted to say.

I was glad that, just then, Mama smiled and said, "You just be as friendly and polite as you can be and things will be fine." She patted my behind and walked over to kiss Billie. Papa leaned over my bed. I put my arms around his neck, and he kissed me on my nose.

"Lights out now," he said, flicking the switch.

After they left, I whispered, "What did Papa say to you?"

"He told me to look out for you," Billie said and turned to face the wall.

Papa didn't have to say that. Billie would look after me anyway. Besides, I could take care of myself. And how could there be trouble? They were just kids, like us. I turned over and wished for morning, when I could put on my new plaid dress with the crisp white collar.

* * *

In the morning, Mama and Papa didn't say anything else about trouble. Before Papa left for work, he just said, "You have a good day, now." I figured they had talked last night and decided there wasn't anything to worry about.

I felt like a queen in my new dress, and was in heaven when Mama cut two pieces of blue ribbon for the ends of my pigtails. "I don't know why I bother with these," she sighed, tying them on. "They'll be lost by the end of the day." She was probably right. That's why she put rubber bands on underneath. But I decided to try real hard to make it through the whole day with both bows.

Before we left, Mama stood Billie and me in front of a mirror in the dining room and said, "You two look so grown up." She sounded a little sad.

Billie smiled, proud. He did look older, taller, and I was almost as tall as him. Mama was tall for a woman, people said. I guess I got it from her. Billie was wearing gray pants and a light blue shirt. Our clothes sort of matched, but I would never say so. Billie'd have a fit.

On my way out the front door, I remembered to peek out through the screen to check for Old Hairy. If there was going to be any trouble, I figured it would come from him, not Parkview folks. The coast was clear.

At the bus stop, Mo spun around to show me her dress. It was glorious, with a green hair ribbon to match.

"Wow! The ribbon goes with your eyes," I said, then showed her mine.

Alice had on a red and gray striped jumper with a white blouse. She kept tugging at her collar, but she looked good.

Fitch and Owen both had on brown pants, but different shirts. They never dressed exactly alike, like some twins. Mr. and Mrs. Sherman said they wanted Fitch and Owen to grow up to be two people, not one.

Everybody looked real nice in their first-day clothes. Even Dillon's cowlick was slicked down and staying—until about lunch time, I figured.

"Think there'll be a ball game at recess on the first day?" Luke asked. "I brought my glove. Did you?"

Everybody had.

"I didn't bring the bat," Billie said. "There'll probably be one at Parkview."

"We're lucky we even *have* a bat after yesterday," Fitch said loudly. Then he turned to Luke, teasing. "Hey, how come Meg risked her neck to save our bat from Old Hairy and all you could do was save yourself?"

The bat belonged to everybody. We'd all chipped in the summer before, after Billie's and then Luke's bat had been broken. We took turns keeping it at home.

"Yeah, Cleary," Billie joined in. "I think my little sister must have more guts than you."

I didn't like being called little, but I couldn't help smiling. I don't know what made me stop for the bat. I was as scared of Hairy as everybody else.

Luke flapped his arms and clucked like a chicken. Then he punched me lightly on the shoulder and said, "That *was* pretty cool, Meg."

He and Alice boosted me up on Billie's shoulders like they do to heroes. I felt like a million bucks.

❧ Chapter Four

The woods and twisty roads of Mayfield soon disap-
peared behind us as the school bus turned onto streets
lined with sidewalks and new brick houses with grass so
perfect it didn't look real. Parkview School was big and
new and crowded with kids, all talking at once. Some
were staring as we got off the bus, or pointing and saying
that we were "the new kids from Mayfield."

"See you at lunch," Alice said as she went off with Fitch
and Owen to the fifth grade.

While Luke and Dillon were looking for the sixth-
grade rooms, Billie squeezed my shoulder and asked,
"You gonna be okay?"

Most times, I liked the way he looked after me, but I
was in the fourth grade now and ready to take care of
myself. I didn't want to hurt his feelings, so I just gave
him the thumbs up sign, grabbed Mo's arm, and headed
down the hall.

"If you need me, I'll be in Room 6A," he called after me.

"Okay," I said without looking back.

When we got to our classroom, there were name cards on each desk so we'd know where the teacher wanted us to sit. I looked at Mo's face three rows away and could see she was as disappointed as I was.

It was just like Papa said. But I also remembered he had said to try to see it as a chance to make new friends, so I decided to make the best of it.

As the desks filled up, I realized that Papa had been right about something else, too. I was the only Negro in the class. I still didn't understand why Papa seemed so worried about it. There hadn't been many Negroes at Mayfield either—Billie and me, the Shermans, and a few others—and we never had trouble with the kids there.

But Papa had said, "Every place isn't like the Crossing. Mayfield is special." I looked over at Mo. Not counting family, I was closer to her than anybody.

I glanced at the girl with short blonde hair seated across the aisle. She didn't see me. I read her name card— IVY SCOTT. Ivy. She reminded me of Dillon without the cowlick. From what I could see, her eyes were blue like his, too.

A boy wearing thick glasses and a shirt that looked real starched was in the seat behind her. When he leaned forward to say something to Ivy, his hand covered his name card.

I was trying to see the name of the girl with brown curls in front of me when the boy behind me pulled my pigtail. It didn't really hurt, and kids at Mayfield did that all the time, mostly if they liked you. I turned around and smiled at a head of straight black hair. He was looking in the other direction, like it was somebody else who'd done it. CLAYTON REED, his card said. He looked big for a fourth grader. The teacher started talking just then, so I faced the front.

"Welcome to Parkview School," the man said, adjusting his glasses. "I'm Mr. Stanley, and I hope you're all as excited as I am to be here." He looked real young for a teacher, younger than Papa.

"The beginning of a school year always offers new possibilities," he said, "a fresh start on things. But this is an extra special year for Parkview."

Mr. Stanley had a friendly face, but he seemed nervous. Like he might not remember all of the speech he'd prepared.

"Some new students have entered our school. Students from a little town called Mayfield Crossing."

Some kids looked around at me. I glanced over at Mo and saw kids had turned and looked at her, too.

"They will feel a bit uncomfortable at first. Everyone does in a new place." Mr. Stanley walked down Mo's aisle. "But the rest of us can do a lot to help the new students in this class, and throughout the school, feel welcome."

He put his hand on top of a boy's head and turned it away from Mo. Other kids who had been staring turned to face the front.

"There's a lot we can learn from each other," Mr. Stanley said.

It sounded so much like something Papa might say that I was beginning to feel right at home.

It was great to see the rest of the gang at lunchtime. Only six people fit at a table, and Mo and I were the last to arrive, so we said hello to everybody and took the nearest seats we could find at a table with some Parkview kids.

"Hi," I said as we sat down. "I'm Meg Turner and this is . . ."

Before I could finish, all four kids picked up their lunches and, without a word, got up and left.

"Hey, what's . . . ?" I started to say, but they were gone.

"Maybe they're in fifth or sixth grade," Mo said. "A girl told me this morning that the big kids here don't like to hang around with the littler kids."

I strained to get a better look at them as they sat down a few tables away. They didn't look that old to me.

"That doesn't make any sense at all," I said.

I caught Billie's eye, and he came over.

"What happened with those kids?" he asked.

By the time Mo had finished telling it, Luke, Alice, Dillon, and the twins had come over, too.

"You guys aren't going to stop talking to us, are you, just 'cause you're older?" Mo asked.

"Don't be dumb," Luke said. He spit in his hand. We all did the same, then joined in one big handshake, and swore that we'd stay friends.

Mo was sure those kids left because we were fourth graders, but later, at recess, we all found out different.

A big kid from Parkview called, "Game!" and everybody headed down toward the ball field to pick up teams. This was what we'd been waiting for. We grabbed our ball gloves and followed the other kids down toward the chain-link backstop behind home plate.

Billie and Luke figured they wouldn't get to be captains right off, seeing that they were new.

"Maybe not," I said, poking Billie, "but wait 'til they come up against the Untouchable Turner."

"Luke the Duke is gonna clean up," Owen said. "And Fitch'll hang 'em out to dry, iron 'em, and stack 'em in neat little piles."

"Yeah? And what are you gonna do, Owen?" Alice said, laughing.

For the first time in his life Owen surprised us all.

"I'm gonna sit this first one out," he said. "I wanna check out the new players."

He sounded cool saying it, but there was something else in his voice, something unsure. I tugged my pigtail. Fitch playing ball with Owen on the sidelines? It wouldn't seem right. Fitch put his arm around Owen's neck as we walked along.

The two Parkview team captains were a sixth grader named Judd, and Clayton, that boy who'd pulled my pigtail. They did the hand-over-hand on the bat, same as we did, to decide who got first pick. Judd won, and right away he pointed to a blond boy standing next to him.

"Cool!" the boy said.

Clayton chose a large boy with a crew cut and ears that stuck out.

Next Judd picked a short kid. The boy ran over punching the pocket of his glove. He looked a lot like Judd, so I thought they might be brothers. It was nice of Judd to choose him. Like Fitch would do with Owen.

Then Clayton picked Ivy Scott. She was wearing a nice red jumper with a white blouse and carrying a mitt that looked all oiled and broken in. She bent over and started tying on Keds she had brought. I was impressed and wondered if Mama would let me bring mine. I could see Alice was thinking the same thing. Only she'd probably rather just wear hers—even with a skirt.

Judd chose again. Then Clayton, and by the time it was over all of us Mayfield kids were still standing there without a team. They hadn't even picked Billie or Luke, who were sixth graders. The Parkview kids didn't speak to any of us, or even look at us. Just acted like we didn't exist, like we weren't even taking up space on the planet.

Alice was hot. We all were. But she was the one who lost it.

"Hey!" she hollered. "This ain't right. Don't you know that when you pick up a game, everybody who shows up gets to play? Even if you don't know how good they are? Even if they're not that good?"

"Cool it, Alice," Luke said. "Yelling won't help."

The Parkview kids just started playing their game, still not saying anything to us.

I could tell Billie was as mad as Alice, but he didn't say a word. He just jerked his head to the side, signaling us all to come away from the game. "This field doesn't belong to them," Alice was saying as Luke and Dillon pulled her along with us. "We go to this school now, too, and they're gonna have to learn to share it whether they like it or not." She was so mad she was almost crying.

"You're right," Mo said. "But Luke's right too. Yelling at them won't do any good."

We walked over toward the playground and stopped at the swings. The swings at Mayfield had had wooden seats, worn smooth from years of kids riding. These were a new kind with rubber slings that squeezed together when you sat down. Bum pinchers. I didn't like them. I don't think the rest of the gang did either, but nobody said anything.

I tugged my pigtail and felt only the rubber band holding my hair together. The other ribbon was still there, but hanging untied, like it was too tired to be a bow anymore.

I looked back toward the game. Everything we'd heard about Parkview's ball field was true. It was neat and green and the diamond seemed almost like the ones they had in the big leagues. But just then, I missed Mayfield's dusty, rocky field so much my stomach hurt.

❧ Chapter Five

"You shoulda seen the way they treated us," I told Mama and Papa after school. "It was like we were nothin'."

"Worse than that," Billie mumbled. He had been quiet the whole way on the bus coming home.

Mama poured us each a tall glass of milk and allowed us two chocolate-chip cookies. They were still warm and were loaded with walnuts. She hardly ever let us have sweets before supper. Even Billie started to perk up a little.

"Give it time," Papa said, patting my arm. "We know it's hard, but you have to give people a chance."

They didn't give *us* a chance, I protested to myself, and Mama, as if she'd heard me thinking, said, "Sometimes you have to give others what they won't give you. Sometimes they're just afraid."

I wanted to ask why they would be scared of us, when

Papa pulled Mama onto his knee and said, "These cookies are killers, woman."

"Sure enough," I agreed, hoping for more.

"We'll have to keep them a secret," Billie joined in, finally coming out of his dark mood. "The army might want to draft her as a secret weapon."

Mama laughed and said, "Thank you very much, but no more cookies until later." She slapped Papa's hand and took the plate away. Then she said, a little shy about complimenting herself, "The nuts made a difference, don't you think?"

We all nodded, our mouths full.

"It was lucky that Harry Slater came selling just as I was mixing the dough," she explained.

Billie and I stopped chewing and looked at each other, our eyes wide. Mama had bought the walnuts from Old Hairy! We managed to leave the kitchen fast and ran outside gagging and choking, certain we wouldn't live to see another day. We knew in our hearts that Mama would never want to feed us anything that might be poisoned, but Mama didn't seem to understand about Old Hairy, and we figured she never would.

Old Hairy had been around for as long as I could remember. And for as long as I could remember, seeing him had made me think of nothing else but running, running for my life.

He was big, but he walked lightly, almost like he didn't weigh anything, almost like a ghost. He lived in a little cabin in the woods. That wasn't so unusual. Nobody in Mayfield Crossing had much. Mr. Wood's new Studebaker station wagon was the most exciting thing anybody'd brought home since Mr. Cleary won their color TV in a sweepstakes. Most of the fathers worked in the saw mill. But not Old Hairy. He sold things. Walnuts, berries, and things he made, like foot stools, picture frames, or Christmas wreaths.

"He makes an honest living," Mama would say.

But there was that hatchet. Dillon's brother Lucky, who left Mayfield to join the Navy, and Frank Sherman, who died the same year of pneumonia, told us about Old Hairy and his hatchet a long time ago. They said one day, when they knew Old Hairy was away picking berries, they went to his cabin and peeked in a window.

"There, lying on the table in plain sight, was the sharpest-looking hatchet you ever saw," Frank said.

"And there was hair and blood all over it," Lucky added in a deep whisper.

We were on Clearys' porch at the time and in the dark, shaking in our shoes just listening to them tell it. Nobody talked about what it might mean. We just looked at each other in the moonlight.

I believed every word. We all did. And we believed that if we weren't careful, *our* hair and *our* blood would end up on that hatchet.

I tried to tell Mama about the hatchet, but she only said, "I wish you kids would leave that man alone. You have no business snooping around his house."

I started to say, "I wasn't snooping," but she might have asked who was, so I dropped it.

Fitch and Owen think Old Hairy was the reason Frank died in the first place. They said one night during a storm, Old Hairy showed up at the Shermans' house carrying Frank, soaking wet and passed out from "the demon rum," as the preacher would say. After that, Frank came down with pneumonia and never got better. They think Old Hairy must've done something to make Frank so sick. I didn't want to think about what. I tried not to think about Old Hairy much at all.

But he wasn't easy to forget. The minute you got your mind on something else—say like a bunch of ants having a picnic on a cube of sugar—Hairy'd pop out of nowhere and scare you so your heart'd fly straight up into your throat.

One morning last spring after breakfast, I stepped out the front door and found him asleep on the porch glider. I jumped about a mile into the air and ran inside screaming, "Mama! Papa! Old Hairy. He's—"

"Calm down. He's no one to be afraid of," Mama said,

31

as I grabbed her tight around the waist. She brushed my bangs back with her hand. I could let her do that all day.

"Just let him be. He'll go home soon," Papa said, not even looking away from his newspaper.

I couldn't believe it. How could they be so calm about the Hatchet Man sleeping right on our porch?

I sat down with Mama, outraged. "What's wrong with him? Why isn't he home sleeping in his own bed?"

"There's nothing wrong with Harry. He's an original, that's all," she said, smiling.

"An original? Old Hairy?"

"First of all," Mama said, with a disapproving look, "Harry Slater isn't much older than I am. You don't call me 'Old Mama,' do you?" I shook my head, scared at just the thought of what would happen if I ever did.

"He just looks older because he has gray hair," Mama explained. "His hair was a nice auburn before he went into the Army. But, when he got back after the war, his hair had gone all gray."

"What made it change color?"

"Who knows?" Mama said. "Some terrible things happen in times of war."

"I still don't see why he's an original."

"Well," Mama paused, as if she wanted to make sure she was putting her words together right, then she said, "He has a special talent for making something useful out of what seems to be nothing. Even as a boy he was never afraid to be different. Sometimes he drinks too much but, well, he's always had his own way of living."

I leaned my head on Mama's knee and tried to understand. But all I could do was tug my pigtail and wish Old Hairy's way of living didn't bring him to our front porch.

✺ *Chapter Six*

"You mean you actually *ate* walnuts that Old Hairy touched?" Fitch asked at lunch the next day. We were all squeezed together at one table, and Fitch was looking back and forth from Billie to me trying to decide which one of us looked likely to keel over first.

Billie confessed with a nod, but gave me a look that asked, *Why did you tell them? Nobody but us had to know.*

He was right. It just slipped out when I saw that Mama had put some of the cookies in our lunches.

"We didn't know until it was too late, and we spit them out," I explained, hoping to be redeemed.

"Your mom sure has a thing for Old Hairy," Owen teased.

"Mrs. Turner likes everybody," Mo said, leaning against me. I could always count on her.

"Yeah, and she makes really good cookies," Luke said.

We all looked longingly at the four huge chocolate-chip cookies.

"It's a shame," Alice sighed.

"It's a shame. It's a shame. But no one's to blame," Owen chanted.

"Hey, didn't you say you'd already swallowed some before you spit out the rest?" Luke asked. "And you guys are still alive. You didn't even get sick or anything, did you?"

Billie and I shook our heads.

"Well, maybe they're okay," Luke said, taking off his glasses, but keeping his eyes glued to the cookies. "Maybe Billie's mama is such a good person that the walnuts were purified the minute she touched 'em. Kinda like a small miracle."

We looked at each other. All wanting to believe, but still not sure if we should chance it. Luke had a way of talking you into things you could be sorry for later.

Then Alice said, "Your mama *is* the church-goin'est person I've ever seen."

Without another word we divided the cookies and ate them like there was no tomorrow. None of us had even eaten our sandwiches yet.

"I've been thinking," Billie started to say.

"Look out," Owen cut in, "Big Bill's thinkin'."

"Well, if we finish lunch early and get to the ball field

first, we can pick up a game ourselves and play. We don't need the Parkview kids."

"Yeah," said Luke, "we got along just fine without them before."

Nobody said anything more. Everybody was just rustling waxed paper, considering Billie's idea.

It was then that I heard someone behind me say, "I don't believe this. It's only the second day of school and I've lost my arithmetic book *and* forgotten my lunch."

I turned to see Ivy sitting at the next table where another girl was giving her half a cupcake. Ivy had gotten to the lunch room late, probably because of the book she'd lost, and it looked like everybody at the table had already eaten their sandwiches.

I elbowed Mo and said, "She needs more to eat than that."

"They're Parkview kids. What do we care?" Alice cut in. She was still mad about yesterday.

"Mama feeds hobos and she doesn't even know them," I said. "Besides, that Ivy girl sits right next to me in class, and she seems okay."

Mo shrugged. Alice ripped a bite out of her apple.

I looked at my sandwich. Peanut butter and jelly. I figured everybody liked peanut butter, so I went up to Ivy's table and said, "You can have half my sandwich."

Ivy looked surprised, then she opened her mouth to

say something, but another girl at her table blurted out, "You're crazy if you eat anything that trashy Mayfielder gives you. Who knows where it's been. It could even be rat meat or something."

"Is not," I said. "It's peanut butter and . . ."

"Yeah," said a boy beside Ivy. "You might not live to see the sun rise. Those coloreds are filthy."

Before I could read her face, Ivy turned away, saying, "No, thank you."

"I just thought . . ." I started to say, but I didn't finish. I knew if I said another word, the tears I was holding in would come right out.

As I was leaving, I heard the boy say, "What are you thanking her for, Ivy? She wasn't doing you a favor."

Then I heard commotion at our table and saw Luke, Fitch and Mo holding on to Billie. The look on my brother's face could have scared a dead man. It sure scared me.

I ran over and whispered, "Billie, remember what Papa said."

We got him to sit down, but he kept staring over at Ivy's table, beads of sweat popping out on his forehead.

"I'd like to go over there and show 'em they can't talk to us that way," Alice fumed.

"Me, too," Mo spat. She didn't sound like herself.

Finally, Billie relaxed. "You did right, Meg," he said. "They just don't have any manners."

"Yeah, they ain't worth it," Luke agreed.

"Forget it," I said, knowing I couldn't.

❧ *Chapter Seven*

"I'm the pitcher! Get off my mound!" Clayton Reed shouted to Billie.

We had started a pick-up game after lunch a couple of days later, just like we planned. We had been hanging around the swings, watching the Parkview kids play ball long enough. Today was our turn.

"You deaf or something, tar baby?" Clayton said as he marched across the field with about twenty kids following him.

Papa had warned us about fighting. But I felt sure something awful was about to happen. Billie looked ready to explode, but he didn't make a move. He might have been more afraid of our father than he was mad, but I think he just didn't want to let Papa down.

"I don't see your name on it," Alice announced. "This ball field is everybody's. And right now, we're using it."

"Yeah," Luke said, "First come, first served, so why don't you just get lost so we can finish our game."

"Make us," Clayton said. He hadn't pulled my hair since the first day, but I'd come to know that he had pulled it to be mean, not for fun. Now he was asking for a fight.

I glanced at Mo and could tell she was as scared as I was. We all stood around the pitcher's mound, eyeing each other—Mayfield kids and Parkview kids, waiting for someone to start something.

"Lordy," Dillon exclaimed, pointing toward home plate, "there's Old Hairy." Good ol' Dillon. We all owed him our lives. His eagle eye had saved us from Hairy a thousand times.

Everybody, even the Parkview kids, turned to look. There was Old Hairy, wearing those same faded overalls but a different shirt, watching us through the wire backstop. He looked hot and sweaty, like he'd walked a long way, and he had his knapsack on his back.

"Shoot," Billie said, "how'd he get here?" My brother was right about most things, but he'd been dead wrong about Hairy not finding us at the new school.

"You know that guy?" Clayton asked, forgetting his challenge.

"No," Luke, Fitch, and Alice said all at once.

But it was too late to deny. Dillon had claimed Old Hairy as ours the minute he recognized him. And I could see the sorry in Dillon's eyes. He must have felt as bad as I did telling about the cookies.

"You sure he's not your daddy?" Clayton said, laughing. He studied Hairy a moment, then frowned and said, "Hey, isn't he the Hatchet Man?"

Some other Parkview kids started saying things like, "the Hatchet Man," "He's supposed to be crazy," and "I heard he kills animals with a hatchet and eats them raw." I'd never heard anything like that. How did *they* know about Hairy?

"Figures he'd be from Mayfield." Clayton said. He tried to sound tough, but I could tell he was nervous. Billie picked up on it, too.

"Yeah, Old Hairy's from Mayfield," Billie said. "He keeps his bloody hatchet in that knapsack he's carryin' and he'll use it on more than animals if he has a mind to."

Clayton and the rest of the Parkview kids started to walk out across second base toward the school. "He's nothing but trash, like all you Mayfielders!" Clayton yelled.

"He isn't trash," I called, feeling braver as they hurried off the field. "Old Hairy's an original."

Billie looked at me, surprised, and laughed. "I wish Mama'd heard that."

Luke pulled my pigtail, teasing, and the rest of the Mayfield gang laughed.

They figured I'd said it just to get the last word, and

41

that was mostly true. But part of me was sticking up for Old Hairy because, whether he'd meant to or not, he'd done us a favor.

I looked back across home plate. Old Hairy was gone. I wasn't exactly sorry he'd left, but for the first time in my life I was glad he'd come. And for the first time since we'd come to Parkview, we played a little ball on the thick green grass of our new school field.

❧ *Chapter Eight*

I asked Billie not to tell Mama what I'd said about Old Hairy being an original. If I knew Mama, she might decide to invite him to supper or something. And I still didn't want to come within a mile of him.

That evening Fitch and Owen came to our bedroom window and were talking with Billie and me about school.

"Owen got a hundred percent on a spelling quiz we had today," Fitch told us, standing on tiptoes. Both he and Owen were short, but he was so proud he looked tall just then.

"Fitch only missed two." Owen propped his foot against the house. "It was only a practice test."

"So Miss Derry wrote Owen's name on the board with another kid who'd only missed one," Fitch went on. "A white kid. But the kid stood up and asked her to erase his name."

"Why?" I asked, pulling myself further onto the windowsill. Mrs. Sherman whistled for them to come home, but Fitch and Owen acted like they didn't even hear.

"He made Miss Derry think he was embarrassed to have his name up," Fitch explained. "But I heard him whisper to another white kid that he didn't want to be associated with us. With 'coloreds' is what he said." Fitch broke a stick in half.

It got quiet. There was something hanging in the air. Billie hadn't said a word. Owen had stopped talking, too, so I knew things weren't right. It was scary. We could always talk about things before. But we just stayed there—Billie and me leaning out the window, and Fitch and Owen against the house, watching the sun set. Finally, Mrs. Sherman whistled again, and Fitch and Owen ran home.

Later, in bed, I couldn't stop thinking about Owen. It was awful what had happened to him. But what really kept me awake were those two words—"white kid." I had never heard any of the Shermans talk that way before, or anybody in Mayfield. It gave me a pain in my chest I can't describe.

Next morning after Saturday chores, Billie and I went out to get some of the kids, but the Crossing was deserted. You'd have thought there'd been an air raid. The Clearys were visiting their grandma, Dillon was hunting with his dad, and the twins were grounded for staying out after their curfew the night before.

We wanted to explain to Mr. and Mrs. Sherman that it was partly our fault, that we were talking about something really important. But, on second thought, we knew Fitch and Owen wouldn't want us to. If things had been reversed, we wouldn't have wanted them to. So we went back home.

"Let's work on your village," Billie said.

"Sure enough?" I asked, uncertain that he meant it. Usually I had to beg him to do such things.

When I was little, we used to just make dirt roads for our miniature cars, but then we'd started setting up little houses from Billie's train set and adding some little farm animals I had. Sometimes we used rocks and sticks to stand for things, like corrals or benches. Once we even dug up johnny-jump-ups and buttercups and replanted them to make a park.

Mo and I had done some work the week before and it hadn't rained since then, so Billie and I didn't have to start from scratch. Billie took the toy beach shovel and started to scrape the roads to make them smooth again. I put three cars down on a section he had finished, then decided to make a pool for the park. I dug a hole and fit a jar lid in so the top was even with the ground. I was cleaning up the area around the pool, planning to fill it with water, when a shadow blocked the sunlight.

I looked up. I stopped breathing. Old Hairy was standing right there watching me. He was so close I could have reached out and touched him. Worse than that, he could have touched me.

"Run, Meg!"

I was frozen in place looking straight at Old Hairy. The sun was behind him, so I couldn't see much. Only his big dark shape.

I thought I heard him start to say something just as Billie yanked my arm and we ran toward the house. I fell up the porch steps, climbing the last two on all fours with Billie pushing me from behind.

Then we charged inside, slamming the door behind us, and peeked out a window. Old Hairy just stood there looking at us, then he stooped down by our cars.

"What's he doin'?" I whispered, even though I didn't have to. Papa was at the store and Mama was in the cellar doing laundry.

We couldn't see what Hairy was up to but, at one point, he put his hand in his pocket. Finally, he stood up and looked at the house. Then he lifted his hand, like he did that day he broke up our last game of the summer. We ducked behind the curtains. After a minute, Billie peeked out. "He's leaving. Come on."

"He took our cars!" I exclaimed, dashing with Billie to the scene of the crime.

But I was wrong. Our metal cars were right where we'd left them. On the dirt road behind them were two more cars made of walnut shells. Each had little pencil-eraser wheels with toothpicks for axles. I had never seen anything like them. There was a little red "B" painted on one and a blue "M" on the other.

"Glory," Billie said, scratching his head.

I couldn't help laughing. And I wondered what Old Hairy might have said if I'd stayed to hear.

❧ *Chapter Nine*

"You should have seen her," Dillon said Monday at the bus stop. "She had the biggest, prettiest eyes you ever saw."

"Did you shoot her?" Luke asked, winking at the rest of us. We all knew the answer.

"Naw, we were hunting ground hogs. It won't be doe season for a couple months."

We loved Dillon's hunting stories. As usual, he didn't kill anything. We used to think Dillon just couldn't shoot straight. But we had all come to realize that he would never kill anything on purpose. He just liked going camping with his dad and seeing the animals. The only real shooting he did was with a Brownie camera.

"Oh, no," Mo suddenly moaned, looking at her arms. They were red and splotchy. "I must have gotten poison ivy picking berries at Gram's." She started to twitch. We all knew how it was. Once you know you have it, you feel itchy all over.

When we got to school, Mr. Stanley sent Mo to the nurse. I missed her the minute she left the room.

I caught Ivy's eye. She looked back at Clayton, then faced straight ahead. I wished I knew what she was thinking.

Last Friday, Mr. Stanley had mentioned that we were going to be studying the fifty states. He said we might want to test ourselves over the weekend, just for fun, to see how many state names we could remember.

"I told you Friday that I wasn't going to test you today on the states, and I'm not," he said. "But I thought we'd have a little contest. Don't worry. No grades."

This was my lucky day. The year before, at Mayfield School, our third-grade class learned a song about the states for our spring concert. We practiced that song so many times I was singing it in my sleep.

Even though I knew I could never forget it, I sang it to Mama on Saturday just in case, and I still knew every state in alphabetical order. Then Mo and I sang it again together on Sunday. I felt bad that she wasn't going to be in on the contest.

After we had gotten paper and put our names on it, Mr. Stanley said, "Ready? Begin."

I started with "Alabama" and sang it all the way through in my head, writing as fast as I could.

"Pencils down," Mr. Stanley said just as I was finishing the "g" in Wyoming. "Now," he continued, "the last person in each row, bring your paper to the first person in the row, and everyone else pass your paper to the person behind you."

I tugged my pigtail. Clayton would be checking my paper. Then I relaxed and felt kind of good. It would kill him that I had a perfect paper.

Mr. Stanley started calling off state names in alphabetical order, giving everyone enough time to check through their lists.

The curly-haired girl in front of me, whose name was Jane, had thirty-three states. I thought that was pretty good considering that nobody had really studied. Then I felt a little guilty. Maybe it wasn't fair that I knew that song.

"Mr. Stanley," Clayton suddenly called out. "I think I caught myself a cheater."

Everybody looked at me. I turned toward Clayton. He was grinning like he'd just answered the $64,000 Question.

Mr. Stanley frowned. "Now, wait a minute, Clayton. That's a very serious accusation."

"I know, sir," Clayton replied. "But she must have a cheat sheet because they're all in alphabetical order. She wasn't even smart enough to mix them up." Mr. Stanley was standing right beside us by then and Clayton handed him my paper.

He looked at the paper and asked, not like he was accusing me or anything, "Margaret, would you like to tell us your side of this?"

I wanted to, but I was so mad, I knew I'd cry if I opened my mouth. My eyes were already filling up. Mr. Stanley must have seen because he touched my shoulder and led me out of the classroom. Before the door closed, some kids were talking and I heard someone say, "That dumb Mayfielder's in for it now."

Mr. Stanley stuck his head back in the door and shushed the class. Then he gave me his handkerchief. It was so clean and fancy with a blue "S" sewn on it, I felt funny about using it. "Don't worry," he said, "I have eleven more just like it."

I smiled a little and blew my nose.

"Now," he said, "tell me."

"I don't know. Maybe it *was* cheating," I said. Then I told him about the song.

Mr. Stanley chuckled, put his hands on my shoulders, and said firmly, "You did *not* cheat, Meg. Cheating involves dishonesty. Something you learned in the past paid off today, that's all. And you can feel good about that."

"Mo Cleary knows the song, too," I said, not wanting to take all the credit.

"Well, then, you both should feel proud," Mr. Stanley

said. "And your teacher would be proud that you remembered something good from last year. Every teacher wants that."

I handed him his handkerchief, and he stuck it right back in his pocket, even though I'd blown my nose on it.

I went back to my seat and Mr. Stanley explained the whole thing to the class.

Clayton whispered, "You dirty liar." Then he raised his hand and said, "Mr. Stanley, do you think she could sing this song for the whole class? Maybe we'd *all* like to learn it."

My face got hot. It was a challenge, I knew. Mr. Stanley knew it, too.

"If you're asking Margaret to prove herself, I don't think that's necessary."

I was glad that Mr. Stanley believed me, but I wanted to show that Clayton Reed. "I don't mind singing it," I said.

Mr. Stanley nodded.

I marched to the front of the classroom and sang the whole song. Not just the states part, but all the rest about the fifty states being from thirteen original colonies, about the fifty stars in the flag and everything. I sang the best I could, with feeling, like my music teacher always told us to. And when I finished, everybody clapped.

It was clear that I had won the contest. Mr. Stanley gave me a jigsaw puzzle of the fifty states.

"I wish I had one for Mo. I must say, I wasn't prepared for you two," he said, laughing.

As I walked back to my desk, I looked right at Clayton and kept staring at him. His face was redder than I thought a person's could get. I flashed him a fake smile before sitting down.

"Clayton, I believe you owe Margaret an apology," Mr. Stanley said. "Normally I would ask that you do it privately, but your accusation was a public one; therefore, your apology should be also."

There was a long silence. Then Clayton, looking at his desk top the whole time, mumbled, "Sorry I said she was cheating."

"Don't tell *me*. Tell *her*," Mr. Stanley insisted.

Clayton sighed. I almost felt sorry for him. It was like it was the hardest thing he ever had to do.

"Sorry I said you were cheating," he finally said.

He never looked at me or said my name, but I knew it was the best I'd get, so I said, "Okay."

Mr. Stanley started pointing out states on a huge map on the wall. I was glad we were getting back to normal.

I was putting my puzzle away when I saw Ivy looking at me, and this time she didn't turn away. She smiled. It was a shy smile, like she wasn't sure how I felt. I smiled back, and hoped she'd know.

But the good feeling was ruined by Clayton, who leaned forward, pulled my pigtail hard, and said, "Just wait until recess."

🍂 Chapter Ten

"He apologized in front of the whole class?" Mo asked with a grin, as we hurried out for recess. Her arms were pink with calamine lotion.

I was telling her all about the contest, and keeping a lookout for Clayton. I didn't know what he'd do, but whatever it was, I didn't want it to come by surprise.

It did anyway. I turned my head to check behind me and the next thing I knew Mo was shouting, "Meg! Look out!" and I hit the ground. Clayton had rammed right into me. He moved like he was going to jump on me, but I got to my feet and ran. I was a pretty fast runner and it helped that I was scared. But Clayton's legs were longer and he was as mad as I was scared. I could hear his shoes pounding the ground behind me, and gaining. Finally, he got close enough to grab one of my pigtails and put me on the ground again. It hurt so bad I forgot everything Papa had said and was ready to fight back.

Clayton started to come at me and I was putting my feet up to kick him off, when somebody jumped on him from behind. It was Billie. They both fell over, then they got to their feet and stood, fists up, yelling at each other.

"Wanna fight somebody?" Billie shouted, "I'll fight you. But lay another hand on my sister and I'll kill you."

"I'll do what I want to your pickaninny sister, and I'll beat the black offa you, too!" Clayton hollered.

Billie went in swinging and Clayton started punching back.

By now, kids had gathered and were screaming. And I was feeling scared for Billie. Not that he'd get hurt bad, but that if somebody didn't stop him, maybe he *would* kill Clayton. He was madder than I'd ever seen him.

"Billie!" I cried, trying to get up, hurting all over.

"Here comes Mr. Perkins!" someone called. "Mrs. Carmichael, too!"

Clayton stopped throwing punches the second he heard that teachers were coming, but Billie either hadn't heard or didn't care. He belted Clayton in the stomach and started to hit him again, but I ran to Billie, threw my arms around him from behind, and held on.

He was trembling, then in an instant I felt him relax and he turned around and hugged me tight. My back hurt from the fall, but I didn't care. I could have stood there being held forever if Mr. Perkins hadn't grabbed Billie's shirt collar and shouted, "Hey, boy! Just what do you think you're doing?"

One of Billie's buttons popped off.

"Hey!" I couldn't help saying and stooped down to pick it up from the ground. I wanted to say more, but I stopped myself. I knew Mama and Papa would skin me alive for being disrespectful. Still, it didn't seem right that Mr. Perkins should be so rough with Billie. Like he was some kind of criminal.

Clayton was bent over holding his stomach, and talking to Mrs. Carmichael.

Mr. Perkins yanked Billie's shirt again, then grabbed my arm with his other hand and said, "You two need to have a talk with the principal."

"You had better come too, Clayton," Mrs. Carmichael said, patting his shoulder.

"Yes, ma'am," Clayton said, acting as innocent as a preacher's son.

As they took us into the school building, Mr. Perkins said to Mrs. Carmichael, "Do you want to bet this won't be the first time something like this happens?"

She nodded and said, "I knew these Mayfield kids would be nothing but trouble."

They expected us to be bad, just like Mrs. Sherman had said. It wasn't right. I held back a sob, but couldn't stop the tears.

* * *

"This is a school, *not* a war zone," Mr. Callahan, the principal, told us from behind his huge desk. "Now, what started this?"

"He threatened to kill me," Clayton blurted out, which wasn't exactly true. Then he *really* lied and made it sound like we ganged up on him.

"I was just walking, minding my own business, when that . . . that boy," he said, pointing to Billie, "jumped on my back. Then after I was down, his sister kicked me in the stomach, so I fought back. It was self-defense."

"Why would they attack you?" Mr. Callahan asked.

"Don't ask *me*," Clayton said, throwing his hands in the air. "We never had trouble before those Mayfielders came."

The principal was quiet a minute, then he turned to Billie and me. "Is that the way it happened?"

The two of us just sat there. Telling—even on someone like Clayton—wasn't our way. Mr. Callahan looked at us hard. I could see a big paddle in the corner behind his desk. It looked old and worn like it had swatted a zillion kids. If Parkview was anything like Mayfield, fighting was serious enough for getting the wood.

Finally Billie said, "It won't happen again, Mr. Callahan, sir."

"You are very right about that," he said. "And what about you, Miss Turner? It's bad enough that these boys were fighting, but you're a young lady." When Mr. Callahan frowned, it looked like he had one big eyebrow drawn over his eyes with no space in between.

I tried not to say anything, but I couldn't help it. "Billie was just protecting me," I said.

"Meg," Billie said.

Mr. Callahan shook his head at Billie and said to me, "Go on."

I tugged my pigtail and I looked down at my lap. "In Mayfield . . . we don't tell on each other," I said quietly. "That's why Billie isn't talking."

"I see."

"But it isn't right for Clayton to say what he did either."

Clayton stood up like he was going to argue, but Mr. Callahan put his hand up like a traffic cop and he sat back down.

"I understand how you feel. But it would help if I had all the facts," Mr. Callahan said.

I almost looked at Billie to see if his eyes approved, then I changed my mind. I didn't want to know because I knew I had to tell it anyway.

I took a deep, shaky breath. Then I started with the fifty states and had just gotten to the part where Clayton pulled my hair and knocked me down on the playground, when Clayton blurted out, "She's a filthy liar."

"You're the liar," Billie yelled back.

"Who are you going to believe?" Clayton asked Mr. Callahan. "Me, or them coloreds from Mayfield? Even my father says they're all liars." His voice got quieter at the end, like he might be saying something he shouldn't to the principal.

Mr. Callahan was standing now, his thick eyebrows lower on his forehead. He looked dead at Clayton and said, "Who these children are or where they come from is not a matter of concern to me. What I'm interested in here is the truth."

He sat back down and nodded for me to finish telling what happened. When I got to the end I said, "So Billie wouldn't have been fighting, but well, he's my brother."

Mr. Callahan didn't answer. I figured he didn't want to say it was okay to fight. He couldn't. He was the principal. But I got the feeling that Mr. Callahan understood. He straightened some papers on his desk, thinking. I eyed the wood. He was going to use it. I knew it. We had broken the rules. He didn't have a choice. He picked up the paddle and went into the assistant principal's office. I heard them talking, then Mr. Callahan called us in one by one.

Clayton went first. He got three swats, hard ones, I

could tell. He was bawling when he left. Billie was next. I could hear them talking for a while, then three swats again, but quieter. Billie didn't cry. I knew he wouldn't.

"Miss Turner?" Mr. Callahan said. I was scared, but I wanted to be brave like Billie. I walked in. The assistant principal was leaning back in his desk chair like this was something that happened every day, like the morning announcements or the lunch-time bell.

"How many swats do you think you'll need so that this won't happen again?" Mr. Callahan asked.

I didn't know what to say. At first I thought I didn't need *any* swats. But then I confessed, "Well, I guess I didn't have to sing the fifty states song. I guess I just wanted to make Clayton mad."

"One swat?" Mr. Callahan asked.

I nodded, leaned over with my hands on my knees, and closed my eyes tight while he swung the big paddle. I never thought I'd smile getting the wood, but it felt as light as Mama's hand sending me off to bed.

When I turned around, Mr. Callahan's face was serious, but his eyes were smiling.

"Let *that* be a lesson to you," he said firmly.

I started to say, *That didn't hurt at all!* But he put his finger to his lips like it was a secret.

We walked back through his office to the door. "One more thing," he said.

"Yes, sir?"

He stooped down so I could look straight at him. "Come back and talk to me sometime. I'd like to hear more about Mayfield Crossing."

On the way home from the bus stop, Billie told me Mr. Callahan had asked him the same question about the swats. "I told him I'd take what Clayton got, but I think he went easy on me."

"He sure went easy on *me*," I said, "but I got the feeling that Mr. Callahan wouldn't want us to tell anybody."

"Yeah," Billie agreed. "We shouldn't tell Mama and Papa about the fight, either. It would only get us into more trouble, and they would worry about something they can't do anything about anyway."

He wanted me to swear with a spit handshake not to tell. He said we had to work things out ourselves. I didn't see how we could, but I swore anyway.

It turned out to be a wasted promise because the minute we walked into the house Mama said, "The principal called."

❧ *Chapter Eleven*

"Mr. Callahan explained what happened today," Mama said, stirring a pot of navy beans.

Billie and I looked at each other. We hadn't thought he would, but I guessed it was another one of those things a principal doesn't have a choice about.

"Now," Mama said. She put the lid on the pot and turned to face us. "I want to hear it from you."

I knew what that meant. We'd talk about it, and then we'd get a spanking. It was a standing rule. If we did something bad enough to get paddled at school, then we got it at home, too.

"Just lick us now and get it over with," I said.

Mama brushed my bangs back with her hand and said softly, "I'm not going to spank you. Not after what Mr. Callahan said."

I couldn't believe it. It was a first.

"I just want you to talk to me about this whole situation at Parkview. I know there are things going on that you haven't told me or your father."

"It's okay, Mama," Billie insisted.

Mama looked me right in the eyes. I looked at my shoelaces.

"Please, Mama," Billie begged, "let it be for now."

Mama studied us both for a minute, then she did what Billie asked. She let it be. "For now," she added. I knew that meant we'd have to talk about it when Papa came home.

Billie and I went out and sat on the back porch swing. The Clearys came over to see if we wanted to play ball. Billie just shook his head as Dillon and the twins walked up the porch steps.

"Did you get it again because of the fight today?" Alice was asking. Luke shushed her.

"No," I answered. "Mama said we'll talk about it later."

Everybody had seen most of the fight, but I told them about everything else, except the swats and our secret with Mr. Callahan.

"Wow," Luke said. "I wish our teacher was as nice as yours, Meg. Don't you, Billie?"

"Yeah."

Billie hadn't told me much about Mrs. Carmichael at all, only that she was hard.

"Is she mean?" Mo asked.

"She pretends to be nice," Luke explained. "But you can tell that she doesn't like us Mayfield kids. She said we'll all have to get used to—" he pushed his glasses down and wrinkled his nose to give us a picture of how she looked— *"higher standards.* And it's worse for Billie," he went on, and told all about how their teacher said it wouldn't be so easy for Billie to make A's at Parkview. Luke mocked her using a high, scratchy voice. "But your people have come a long way. I'm sure you'll do fine."

Billie rolled his eyes.

"I get the same feeling from Miss Derry," Alice said, looking at Owen. "When you got the best spelling grade, remember how she checked your paper about three times, like she couldn't believe it?"

"Didn't you tell us she put your name on the board?" I asked.

"Yeah," Fitch said, "but not until after she was sure his mark was for real. She even asked him to spell two of the hardest words out loud."

"I knew she was checking to see if I'd cheated somehow, but she tried not to make it seem that way," Owen said. "She just said a lot of people had missed those words and that I should remind the class how to spell them, even though all anybody had to do was check the darn book."

Alice sighed. "Nobody wants us there." She slid her back down the side of the house and sat on the porch floor.

Luke plopped into a lawn chair and stared at the ceiling. Fitch and Owen sat on the top porch step, looking away from the house. Dillon stood behind them, leaning against the side of the house. I was on the porch swing between Billie and Mo. It was dead quiet. Mo put her head on my shoulder.

In a little while she said, "Mr. Stanley's nice."

"And Mr. Callahan," I added.

"And we did get to play on the field the other day," Luke said.

We were all looking for the silver lining in the dark cloud over Parkview School.

After Papa came home, we had our talk. He smiled a little when I told him about what happened with the fifty states, but he said, "It *was* wrong of you to be so smug. It only made matters worse."

"I know, Papa," I said, unable to look at his eyes.

He patted my leg. "Yes, I know you know. Just try not to forget what you've learned."

Then he turned to Billie. "Was there any time during the fight that you could have walked away?"

"He was beating up on Meg, Papa," Billie said.

"Yes, I know. And you were right to defend her. But think about it. Could you have ended it sooner?"

Billie was quiet, then he said, "Yes, sir."

I didn't know what he was talking about. "When?" I asked.

"After I jumped on Clayton and we were yelling at each other. I could have quit, but he said that stuff that made me mad."

I remembered what Clayton had said. People always say words can't hurt you, but that isn't true. They can hurt worse than a punch in the eye.

But Papa understood. He didn't punish us. He said, "You've never had hatred in your hearts. Don't let them put it there now. If you do, then *they* win."

Mama squeezed us both. "You just do what you've always done. Be your best."

Long after bedtime, I still couldn't sleep. I could hear something on television about the election for president. I knew Mama and Papa were hoping a man named Kennedy would win. "He would be good for this country," Mama had said.

If this Kennedy did become president, I wondered if he could come to Parkview and straighten things out.

Maybe. He must be a good man or Mama and Papa wouldn't vote for him.

Even though Billie was across the room and facing the wall, I was sure he was awake, too.

"Billie?"

He didn't answer for a while and I thought maybe I was wrong, maybe he *was* asleep. Then he said, "Papa always told us it was wrong to fight, but he never said how right it'd feel to hit somebody like Clayton."

"Did it really feel good?"

"Yeah."

"What are we gonna do, Billie?"

"We'll work it out."

"But how? How can we work it out with kids who think we're trash?"

"I'm not sure," he whispered, turning over to face me in the dark. "But Papa's right. It's not right for us to be hatin' them and them to be hatin' us."

We were quiet for a bit. I got this picture in my head of what it could be like if we all got along.

"Wouldn't it be great if we could play a real game of baseball with the kids from Parkview?"

"Yeah." It was quiet again, then suddenly Billie sat up and said, "Maybe we can, Meg."

"Are you kids still awake in there?" Mama called.

I waited until I knew Mama wasn't listening anymore

and whispered, "What are you talking about? How're we gonna get them to play *us?*"

"Let me think," Billie said with hope in his voice. "We'll talk about it tomorrow."

I heard Owen's voice echo in my head. *Look out. Big Bill's thinkin'.*

I pulled the covers up and closed my eyes tight. Mama always said just wishing a thing wouldn't make it happen, but I figured with me wishing and Billie thinking, anything might.

❧ *Chapter Twelve*

When I woke up, Billie's bed was made and he was gone. Mama said he'd gotten ready for school early and gone over to Clearys'.

Shoot, I thought. I hadn't heard a thing. When he wanted to, Billie could be quieter than a cat. I was dying to know what he was planning. I got dressed as fast as I could and started to rush out, but Mama called me back for breakfast.

"Aw, Mama, just this once." I stood at the table and gulped down my juice, ready to make my escape.

Papa folded down his newspaper and gave me *the look*. It was a warning.

I sat down and ate my cereal. Papa nodded and went back to his paper. When I'd finished, Mama kissed my forehead and hugged me.

"You take care today, you hear?"

"Yes, ma'am," I answered, as she handed me my lunch and shooed me out the front door.

One step later I caught my breath and jumped back inside. Old Hairy was asleep on the porch again. What did he think this was, a hotel?

Mama had already gone back into the kitchen, and I started to run after her. But something made me go back and peek at Hairy through the screen door. He looked funny, sort of smiling in his sleep, but snoring like a freight train. At the same time he seemed peaceful, lying in the shade of Mama's pretty purple morning glories strung from the porch rail, with his hands folded together on his belly.

I opened the door quietly and tiptoed right up next to him. There were some reddish-brown stains on his hands, and for a second I thought it might be blood. But he smelled a little like turpentine, so I figured it was the varnish he used for his wood crafts. He smelled like sweat and whiskey, too, and he *was* hairy, but he didn't really look like a werewolf. His whiskers looked soft and shiny, like if I touched them they'd feel like silk. Still, if he had opened his eyes, I might've died of fright.

I squeezed my own eyes shut and slowly opened my lunch bag. I reached inside, wishing that paper bags didn't make so much noise, that I could be as quiet as Billie. After what seemed like a hundred minutes, I finally pulled out my peanut butter sandwich. I put it right beside Hairy, near his face so he'd see it when he woke up. Then I ran to the bus stop.

"Meg really gave me the idea," Billie was saying when I arrived.

"What idea?" I wanted to know.

"We're going to challenge Clayton and the Parkview kids to a baseball game," Luke said.

"They'll never play us," Alice grumbled, shaking her head. I was thinking the same thing. They didn't want to play ball with us before, why would they now?

"Yes, they will," Billie insisted. "Because we won't be asking to play *with* them. We're gonna tell them we want to play *against* them for the school championship."

"Yeah," Dillon said, smiling. "They'll have to agree or it will look like they're scared we might beat 'em, which we will."

"Even if they *do* play us, how's that gonna change anything?" I asked. "If we win, they'll hate us more, and if we lose they'll make fun of us worse than ever."

"I don't think so, Meg," Billie said. "If we win, maybe they won't like us, but they'll have to respect us, and that's somethin'."

"What if we lose?" Owen asked.

"Don't know. It's a risk, I guess. And maybe everybody doesn't wanna take it."

"We should vote," Mo said.

"Okay," Luke asked with his hand already in the air. "How many want to challenge the Parkview kids to a championship game, win or lose?"

Billie's hand was up right away, along with Dillon's. I looked at Mo and we raised ours together. Alice's was up and waving. We all faced the twins.

Fitch looked like he wanted to go along, but he held back, studying Owen. I knew what was happening. Fitch knew that Owen would do what he did, but he also figured that Owen was scared to play. He didn't want to hurt our chances of winning.

I could tell Owen wanted to play, and I wanted him to. It wouldn't seem right without us all together.

"Come on, Owen," I said. "Remember what you said— 'We're gonna hang 'em on the line, press 'em, and stack 'em up high'?"

Owen laughed. "No," he said, "it's—'hang 'em out to dry, iron 'em, and stack 'em in neat little piles.'"

Fitch slapped Owen's back, grabbed his hand and raised it high in the air.

It looked like we were gonna play some ball.

❧ *Chapter Thirteen*

"So what do you say?" Billie asked Clayton at recess. "Do you want to play us for the school championship or not?"

As usual, we were divided, with Mayfield kids standing behind Billie on one side of the pitcher's mound and Parkview kids behind Clayton on the other.

Clayton stood glaring. I could tell he didn't trust us.

"Forget it," Luke said, signaling us to walk away. "He's scared of losin'."

We played along and started to leave, knowing Clayton would have to agree now. It was like one of those duels in the Three Musketeers' time. If someone slapped you in the face with a glove, you had to fight, even if you knew you'd get killed or you didn't feel like killing anybody. In those days, it was better to die because you were brave than to live because you were chicken.

"Okay," Clayton finally said. "We'll play. But this is

going to be a real championship game, so everything has to be by the rules."

"That's the way we want it," Billie said. "Fair."

We decided to play the game on Saturday afternoon on the school ball field, figuring we could get somebody's mom or dad to drive us over from the Crossing. I was hoping to get another ride in Mr. Wood's new Studebaker.

That afternoon we met at the old Mayfield School field to practice. First we had to decide what positions people would play.

"We only have eight players," Dillon reminded everyone.

"It doesn't matter," Alice declared. "We could beat them with seven."

We all cheered in agreement.

I'd play my usual position as catcher and Billie would pitch. Luke would play first base, with Dillon on second, and Owen on third, right beside Fitch who would be shortstop. Alice was to cover right field and Mo, left. The center field position was left open. Billie figured Dillon could help cover center, since he could run and could handle grounders. But Dillon wasn't sure. Fly balls were his weakness.

"I don't know, Billie," he said. "Maybe we should put Mo here. She's good with flies."

"Mo can play a little toward center, but you'll be okay,

Dillon," Billie said without a bit of question in his voice. "Don't worry."

We practiced every day that week after school. On Friday, Papa and Mr. Cleary came and hit some balls for us to field, and they substituted for players who were practicing their batting. Papa was slamming balls all over the place, giving everybody a chance to make a play.

When we went home that night, Papa helped us oil our gloves. Then after supper, Mama poured grape juice into four fancy glasses.

"To a good game tomorrow," Papa toasted.

We clinked our glasses together. "A good game," we all said, and drank. We were as ready as we were going to be.

On Saturday morning, Dillon's dad drove us to Parkview in his Studebaker, and I even got to ride up front next to the window. My pigtails were flying in the wind, and by the time we reached Parkview, I was ready to win that game.

"Are you sure you don't want me to stay to cheer you on?" Mr. Wood asked.

"No thanks, Dad," Dillon said.

We had all asked our parents not to come to watch. They would just make us nervous.

We piled out of that shiny new car and walked across

the field to the pitcher's mound to meet with Clayton and his team and decide who'd be batting first.

It looked like the whole school had turned out. There were kids all over the bleachers and standing around the edge of the field.

Clayton tossed the bat and Billie caught it to start the hand-over-hand. Whoever was left holding the end could bat first.

"Hey, wait a minute. Wait just one *cotton pickin' minute,*" Clayton said loudly, smiling in a mean sort of way. Some kids on his team snickered.

"Didn't we say this game was going to be by the rules?" he said. "Don't you know anything at all about baseball?"

"What in blazes are you talking about?" Billie asked.

Clayton looked at some of the Parkview kids and smiled. "You can't play an official baseball game with only eight players."

Billie wiped the sweat from his forehead. "We're willing to play with a handicap and call it even."

"Doesn't matter what you're willing to do, Billie Boy. The rules say nine players. If you can't come up with nine in"—he looked at his watch—"ten minutes, then you forfeit, and *we* win."

"Yeah!" some Parkview kids yelled, but only some. Most were quiet, waiting to see what would happen next.

Someone on the bleachers yelled, "Aw, man! What *is* this?"

Another kid hollered, "On with the game!"

Clayton turned around and shouted, "Rules are rules!"

Billie motioned us to walk over toward third base with him. We huddled together.

"Anybody got any ideas?" he asked.

"We shoulda figured he'd pull somethin' like this," Alice said.

"Yeah, but right now we have to think what to do about it," Billie said.

I figured it was all over until my eye caught motion behind the backstop. It was Old Hairy. Before I even thought about it I said, "What if we ask Hairy?"

Everybody looked at me like I'd invited Frankenstein to dinner.

"Are you crazy, Meg?" Luke said, half laughing. "What's the matter with you?"

"Remember how fast he took the bases that time? He *is* from Mayfield, and I don't mind askin' him."

Everybody was protesting until Billie said, "Anybody got a better idea?"

Nobody said anything. I tugged my pigtail and started to walk toward the backstop. Suddenly I was feeling scared. It was like the Three Musketeers thing again. I didn't really know what Old Hairy would do, but I would rather face a bloody hatchet than forfeit the game to Clayton Reed.

Just then Clayton stepped in front of me. "Where do you think you're going?" He looked over his shoulder at Hairy. "No way!" he said. "No grown-ups."

"That's not an official baseball rule," Fitch said, as the gang gathered around again. The Parkview players came close enough to hear, but they kept watching Hairy.

"You said a fair game," Clayton insisted. "What if I knew Mickey Mantle and brought him along? Would that be fair?"

We hated to admit it, but Clayton was right. It wouldn't be fair for a grown-up to play. Even Hairy.

Billie looked at his watch, then at us. His eyes said he was sorry, as if all this was his fault.

I looked across the field toward the bleachers. There were kids everywhere. Parkview kids.

I caught myself wishing again, even though I knew just wishing a thing wouldn't make it happen. *You have to make things happen*, Mama'd say. *Sometimes you have to take chances.*

Billie sighed and turned to Clayton, who hadn't stopped smiling since he walked onto the field, held out his hand, and said, "Well, it looks like we'll have to . . ."

"Wait!" I yelled. And I ran toward the bleachers, toward that head of short blond hair that reminded me so much of Dillon.

"Ivy?" I said. I didn't have to shout. I could tell she'd seen me coming and was looking right at me from the second row of the bleachers. Billie and Clayton and the whole gang had run over behind me.

"Ivy?" I said again.

Ivy glanced at a girl sitting next to her. The girl frowned and mouthed the words, "No way."

Ivy looked down at the ball glove in her hand.

It was so quiet I could hear my heart beating.

"She's not going to play for *you*," Clayton said, laughing.

Ivy punched the pocket of her glove, looked up at Clayton, and said, "Wanna bet?" She jumped down from her seat in the bleachers, ran over to Billie, and said, "I can play the outfield."

"You can't!" Clayton yelled, pushing some kids aside to stand in front of her. "You said you didn't want to play ball today."

"I changed my mind," Ivy said calmly.

Clayton kept hollering. "This is supposed to be Parkview kids against Mayfield kids. The championship. You *can't* play for them."

"Clayton," Ivy said, turning toward us, "Mayfield kids *are* Parkview kids."

"Yeah!" Mo and I cried together. Mo took her ball cap off and plunked it down on Ivy's head. Ivy flashed her that shy smile, same as she did me that day in class, then she reached up, grabbed the brim of the hat and pulled it down over one eye.

Billie smiled at Ivy and punched her lightly on the shoulder. Then he looked at his watch and said to Clayton, "Time to play ball."

A couple of kids on the bleachers yelled, "Traitor," as Ivy ran onto the field, but some were clapping and cheering. They had come out today for the same thing we had, a ball game.

Clayton asked for five minutes to talk to his team and looked grateful when Billie agreed. It sounded like he was deciding who would play what position. I realized then that Clayton had known all along that we only had eight players. He hadn't planned on playing the game from the beginning.

While we waited, Billie dusted my catcher's mitt with a couple of fast balls, then Luke hit a hot line drive straight to center field.

"I got it," Ivy called, and she did.

"Good catch," Alice yelled.

"She's Ivy, but she sure ain't poison," Owen chattered.

"You got that right," a boy from Parkview joined in.

The Untouchable Turner had Fitch swinging at air, but finally he hit a grounder that took him to second base. Dillon warmed up on deck.

"They're pretty good," I heard a girl on the bleachers say, as Billie pitched another Turner.

I felt like jumping clean to the sky. I hardly even cared who won anymore because I knew there'd be other games—lots of them.

I was scooping up a ball that had gotten away from me when I got a glimpse of Hairy standing behind the back-stop.

I pushed back my catcher's mask and looked him right in the eyes. The sunlight was shining just right, and I could see they were a pretty green color. "Hey, Mr. Slater," I said, putting my hand up. Harry smiled and raised his.

I pulled my mask back down and threw the ball to Billie. He was shaking his head and laughing, saying, "Wait 'til I tell Mama."

"No, Billie," I said. "Wait 'til *I* tell her."

Read All the Stories by
Beverly Cleary

☐ **HENRY HUGGINS**
70912-0 ($4.50 US/ $6.50 Can)

☐ **HENRY AND BEEZUS**
70914-7 ($4.50 US/ $6.50 Can)

☐ **HENRY AND THE CLUBHOUSE**
70915-5 ($4.50 US/ $6.50 Can)

☐ **ELLEN TEBBITS**
70913-9 ($4.50 US/ $6.50 Can)

☐ **HENRY AND RIBSY**
70917-1 ($4.50 US/ $6.50 Can)

☐ **BEEZUS AND RAMONA**
70918-X ($4.50 US/ $6.50 Can)

☐ **RAMONA AND HER FATHER**
70916-3 ($4.50 US/ $6.50 Can)

☐ **MITCH AND AMY**
70925-2 ($4.50 US/ $6.50 Can)

☐ **RUNAWAY RALPH**
70953-8 ($4.50 US/ $6.50 Can)

☐ **RAMONA QUIMBY, AGE 8**
70956-2 ($4.50 US/ $6.50 Can)

☐ **RIBSY**
70955-4 ($4.50 US/ $6.50 Can)

☐ **STRIDER**
71236-9 ($4.50 US/ $6.50 Can)

☐ **HENRY AND THE PAPER ROUTE**
70921-X ($4.50 US/ $6.50 Can)

☐ **RAMONA AND HER MOTHER**
70952-X ($3.99 US/ $4.99 Can)

☐ **OTIS SPOFFORD**
70919-8 ($3.99 US/ $4.99 Can)

☐ **THE MOUSE AND THE MOTORCYCLE**
70924-4 ($4.50 US/ $6.50 Can)

☐ **SOCKS**
70926-0 ($4.50 US/ $6.50 Can)

☐ **EMILY'S RUNAWAY IMAGINATION**
70923-6 ($4.50 US/ $6.50 Can)

☐ **MUGGIE MAGGIE**
71087-0 ($4.50 US/ $6.50 Can)

☐ **RAMONA THE PEST**
70954-6 ($3.99 US/ $4.99 Can)

☐ **RALPH S. MOUSE**
70957-0 ($4.50 US/ $6.50 Can)

☐ **DEAR MR. HENSHAW**
70958-9 ($3.99 US/ $5.50 Can)

☐ **RAMONA THE BRAVE**
70959-7 ($3.99 US/ $4.99 Can)

☐ **RAMONA FOREVER**
70960-6 ($4.50 US/ $6.50 Can)

Buy these books at your local bookstore or use this coupon for ordering:
....
Mail to: Avon Books, Dept BP, Box 767, Rte 2, Dresden, TN 38225   E
Please send me the book(s) I have checked above.
❏ My check or money order—no cash or CODs please—for $_____is enclosed (please
add $1.50 per order to cover postage and handling—Canadian residents add 7% GST).
❏ Charge my VISA/MC Acct#_____Exp Date_____
Minimum credit card order is two books or $7.50 (please add postage and handling
charge of $1.50 per order—Canadian residents add 7% GST). For faster service, call
1-800-762-0779. Residents of Tennessee, please call 1-800-633-1607. Prices and numbers are
subject to change without notice. Please allow six to eight weeks for delivery.

Name_____
Address_____
City_____State/Zip_____
Telephone No._____   BEV 0196

WORLDS OF WONDER
FROM
AVON CAMELOT

THE INDIAN IN THE CUPBOARD
Lynne Reid Banks   60012-9/$3.99US/$4.99Can

THE RETURN OF THE INDIAN
Lynne Reid Banks   70284-3/$3.99US only

THE SECRET OF THE INDIAN
Lynne Reid Banks   71040-4/$3.99US only

BEHIND THE ATTIC WALL
Sylvia Cassedy   69843-9/$3.99US/$4.99Can

ALWAYS AND FOREVER FRIENDS
C.S. Adler   70687-3/$3.50US/$4.25Can

Avon Camelot Presents
Award-Winning Author

THEODORE TAYLOR

THE CAY 00142-X $4.50 US/$6.50 Can

After being blinded in a fatal shipwreck, Phillip was rescued from the shark-infested waters by the kindly old black man who had worked on deck. Cast up on a remote island, together they began an amazing adventure.

TIMOTHY OF THE CAY

72522-3 $3.99 US/$4.99 Can

The stunning prequel-sequel to *The Cay*.

THE TROUBLE WITH TUCK

62711-6/ $4.50 US/$6.50 Can

TUCK TRIUMPHANT 71323-3/ $3.99 US/$4.99 Can

MARIA 72120-1/ $3.99 US/ $4.99 Can

THE MALDONADO MIRACLE

70023-9/$3.99 US/$4.99 Can

Stories of Adventure From
THEODORE TAYLOR
Bestselling Author of THE CAY

THE OUTER BANKS TRILOGY

STRANGER FROM THE SEA: TEETONCEY
71024-2/$3.99 US/$4.99 Can

Ben O'Neal spotted a body on the sand—a girl of about ten or eleven; almost his own age—half drowned, more dead than alive. The tiny stranger he named Teetoncey would change everything about the way Ben felt about himself.

BOX OF TREASURES: TEETONCEY AND BEN O'NEAL
71025-0/$3.99 US/$4.99 Can

Teetoncey had not spoken a word in the month she had lived with Ben and his mother. But then the silence ends and Teetoncey reveals a secret about herself and the *Malta Empress* that will change their lives forever.

INTO THE WIND: THE ODYSSEY OF BEN O'NEAL
71026-9/$3.99 US/$4.99 Can

At thirteen, Ben O'Neal is about to begin his lifelong dream—to go to sea. But before Ben sails, he receives an urgent message from Teetoncey, saying she's in trouble.